Rooster's Sore Throat

by Rachel Johns
illustrated by Ian Forss

SCHOOL PUBLISHERS

Printed in Mexico

ISBN 10: 0-15-351417-5
ISBN 13: 978-0-15-351417-3

Ordering Options
ISBN 10: 0-15-351212-1 (Grade 2 Advanced Collection)
ISBN 13: 978-0-15-351212-4 (Grade 2 Advanced Collection)
ISBN 10: 0-15-358052-6 (package of 5)
ISBN 13: 978-0-15-358052-9 (package of 5)

1 2 3 4 5 6 7 8 9 10   050   15 14 13 12 11 10 09 08 07 06

Rooster's throat hurt when he crowed.

"I need a rest," he moaned.

"Impossible," said Farmer. "There is no one else to crow early in the morning."

Rooster went to bed.

"You look terrible," said Cow.

"My throat is sore," moaned Rooster. "There is no one else to crow."

"I could crow tomorrow," suggested Cow.

4

The next morning, Rooster stayed in bed. Cow climbed onto Rooster's fence at sunrise and mooed loudly. Farmer woke with a shudder.

"What is that awful noise?" he wondered.

Farmer could not believe his eyes
when he looked out the window.
"That's quite enough, Cow," he called.
"You're not a rooster."

Cow stopped being a rooster.
"Please give Rooster a rest,"
begged Cow. "His throat is sore."
"That's impossible!" answered
Farmer.

Now Cow's throat hurt.

"You look terrible, Cow," said Goat.

"I crowed for Rooster this morning," groaned Cow. "Now my throat hurts."

"I'll crow tomorrow," said Goat.

The next morning, Cow and Rooster stayed in bed. Goat climbed onto the fence at sunrise and bleated loudly.

Farmer could not believe his eyes when he looked out the window and saw Goat.

"Get off that fence, you silly goat," he bellowed.

"Rooster needs a rest," begged Goat.

"That's impossible!" answered Farmer angrily.

The next morning, no one crowed at sunrise. Farmer slept until the middle of the morning. He did not understand how he could have slept so late. Then he remembered that Rooster was sick.

"I have had enough of this,"
Farmer said.

He went to see Rooster. They talked
for a long time. Then Farmer got in his
truck and went to town.

When he returned, he called Cow
and Goat to a meeting. "I have brought
something for you," he said.

Farmer gave each animal an envelope. Cow and Goat opened the envelopes.

"These are bus tickets to the beach," they cried in amazement. "We don't understand!"

"Rooster needs a vacation," said Farmer. "He won't go without you."

"If we go, there is no one else to crow," they exclaimed.

"There is now," smiled Farmer.
He took an alarm clock out of his
pocket. "This rooster won't get a
sore throat."

14

Think Critically

1. What happened in the story when Rooster had a sore throat?

2. How were Cow and Goat alike?

3. How do you know that Farmer felt sorry for the animals, especially Rooster?

4. What "rooster" wouldn't get a sore throat?

5. If you could change the ending, what would happen?

 **Social Studies**

A Farmer's Jobs Write a list of all the jobs a farmer might need to do. Draw a picture of a farmer doing one of the jobs.

 School-Home Connection Think of a song that you know about a farm or an animal and sing it for your family.